The Problem at
Gruff Springs

by

Nikki Nelson-Hicks

An earlier version of this work was published in Once Upon a Six-
Gun released by Pro Se Press 2014

A buttload of trolls were killed in the creation of this work.

ISBN: 978-1-7320967-1-4

Any references to historical events, real people, or real places are
used fictitiously. Names, characters, and places are products of the
author's imagination.

Front cover image by betibup33@gmail.com

First printing edition 2018

Third Crow Press
640 Bradford Drive
Gallatin, TN 37066
thirdcrowpress@gmail.com

Published Works-

Jake Istenhegyi: The Accidental Detective Series
- A Chick, a Dick and a Witch Walked Into a Barn
- Golems, Goons and Cold Stone Bitches
- Boodaddies, Bogs and a Dead Man's Booty
- Fished Eyed Men, Fedoras and Steel-Toed Pumps
- Road Trips, Acid Baths, and One Eyed Bastards
- Corpses, Coins, Ghosts and Goodbyes

The Shrieking Pits
The Galvanized Girl
Gunn Takes a Gander – A Barrington Gunn Caper
The Perverse Muse
A Round for the Holly King
Rumble (Cryptid Clash! Book 5)
What the Armless Guy Said: The Dare Dialogues

Anthologies-
The Adventures of Moose and Skwirl
Capes and Clockwork: Superheroes in the Age of Steam
Legends of New Pulp Fiction
Nashville Noir
Once Upon a Six Gun
Soundtrack Not Included
When the Shadow Sees the Sun – Creatives
Surviving Depression

Acknowledgements

Thanks to my husband, Brian, who said, "You do realize that's a flint lock, right?" and thereby making me redo all the gun stuff.

Thanks to Tommy Hancock, Pro Se Press, who gave me the challenge to write a story where a Wild West Historical Figure does battle with a Fairy Tale Villain for the anthology, Once Upon a Six Gun.

Thanks to my editor, Brenna Hicks, who caught all the weird commas and fought with me about using onomatopoeia.

Thanks to Dead People's Things, a vintage store, where I bought a carte de viste of Allan Pinkerton which has been staring at me the entire time while writing.

Thanks to my Beta Readers who took time out of their lives to read the early versions of this story and encouraged me to not throw it in the trash: David Michael Rose, Todd Keisling (toddkeisling.com/tk), and Tom Scanlon (tomscanlon.net).

Thanks to Paul Bishop (paulbishopbooks.com), an author with an incredibly tight schedule who took time out to read the story and give me an incredibly kind blurb (my first!).

And to Todd Keisling (toddkeisling.com/tk), an author who will break new heights in horror. I am so thankful to have met before he gets too big (KNEEL BEFORE TODD!) and for taking time to read this story, give me advice and a flattering blurb.

And thanks to Pope Clement VIII for sanctifying coffee. CAFFEINATED4LIFE!

The Problem at
Gruff Springs

by

Nikki Nelson-Hicks

For my Dad,
who would've enjoyed the hell out of this story.

Chapter One

A thundering dust cloud stormed into town, scattering wandering chickens in its path and causing shutters to open in curiosity. In the cloud's nucleus was an ordinary stagecoach, hitched to four frothy, sweat coated horses. The coachman, an old ranch hand called Ruddy, swiped at the air with his hat as he pulled the brake. He climbed down and opened the stagecoach door.

"We're here, fellas. Gruff Springs. In record time, too. Check your watches." Ruddy grinned as he pulled down the stairs. "I suspect you owe me double rates as per our agreement."

Inside the cramped car sat two men. One, a giant Swede squeezed up like a hunchback. The other, a Scotsman, wore a bowler hat, a tailored suit from Chicago and sat more comfortably with his black polished boots resting on the other seat.

The Swede looked at the open door with blessed anticipation. "Boss?"

"In a minute." He checked his pocket watch and looked out the carriage window. He took his

2

pipe out from his pocket, filled the bowl with tobacco, tapped it, and lit it.

"Sheriff's office is right over there. The Gruff Hotel is right across the street," Ruddy said, wiping his face with a handkerchief. "So, if you are ready, I'll take your luggage over."

"In a minute."

"That's all well and good, sir," Ruddy blew his nose into a red handkerchief. "But I still need to get the horses fed and brushed. I'm sure you understand, sirs, it was a very hard ride."

Tendrils of smoke slipped through his lips as the man in the bowler hat clamped down on his pipe and pierced through Ruddy with hard, gray eyes. His faint brogue dropped in pitch as well as temperature. "In. A. Minute."

"Ruddy, take the luggage to the Gruff Hotel. I'll make sure to hand over the horses to the stable boy," the Swede said quickly as his boss went back to staring out the window. "Please be extra careful with the gun case."

"Yessir, Mr. Sigerson," Ruddy grumbled as he walked away. "Double rates, hell. I should've asked for triple."

A few more agonizing seconds passed for the Swede as the second man chewed on his pipe and took in the scenery.

Sigerson looked over his boss' shoulder. All he could see were the colorful banners of blue and gold promoting the Elixir Spa and Hotel and all its miraculous water cures. He rolled his shoulders, trying to ease the growing tension in his back, and groaned. "Boss, I don't want to overstep my boundaries, but what are we waiting for?"

"Ah, finally!" His focus sharpened, like a cat seeing fat prey. "See those men there?"

Five men stood outside the Mercantile. One was elderly and balanced himself with a silver headed cane. His two friends, a shorter nervous man with a face like a whippet and a taller, placid man with coiffed blonde hair, stood around him like book ends. Two other men leaned against the wall were dirtier and harder. They wore guns on their belts.

"Who are they?" asked Sigerson

"We're about to find out." The man in the bowler hat slapped his knee. "Let's go."

Chapter Two

"Excuse me! Excuse me!" An elderly man called out to the stagecoach, sidestepping a group of Temperance workers. His cadre of friends following behind was nearly mowed down by a wheelbarrow as they followed him across the street. "Mr. Pinkerton!"

The man in the bowler hat turned towards the voice. He pulled his pipe out of his mouth and smoothed down his graying beard. "It's Agent Pinkerton, sir. How can I help you?"

"Oh, yes. Of course. Agent Pinkerton, permit me to introduce myself. I am Mr. Lucas Mooneyham. I'm a local businessman. This is Mr. Edmund Talley, he runs the local bank. And this is Mayor Darryl Brown. Welcome to Gruff Springs. If we can be of any-"

"How interesting. News does travel fast here." Pinkerton nodded to the two hired gunmen who lingered in the back. "Gentlemen."

The two stared coldly back.

The Swede emerged from the carriage and towered over the men. The welcoming committee stared up at him as he stretched out his strong, muscular arms and shook his head of long blonde hair. He groaned, deep and husky. Mr. Talley's jaw dropped and Mayor Brown subconsciously checked his hair. Pinkerton held back a grin. The Swede always made an impression.

"My associate, Agent Sigerson. Sigerson, our welcoming committee."

"Gentlemen," he said, nodding at them. "Good afternoon."

"I believe in the importance of a polite staff," he said. "Don't you agree, Mayor Brown?"

"I do what I can for my constituents, yes," said Mayor Darryl "Toad" Brown. He smiled his most practiced smile and held out his hand. "I hope you enjoy your stay in Gruff Springs."

"I hope we find what we came for."

The flush in Mr. Mooneyham's face deepened.

And there it is. Pinkerton nodded and smiled with the confidence of someone who has added up a sum of numbers correctly.

"Boss? The sheriff is waiting."

"See what I mean, gentlemen? Politeness," he said and walked across the street to the sheriff's office.

"Well, obviously politeness doesn't extend to himself," Mr. Talley mumbled.

"Gentlemen," Mr. Mooneyham said as he lowered Mayor Brown's still extended hand with his silver tipped cane. "I believe we have a problem."

Chapter Three

Pinkerton swept a critical gaze over the sheriff's office. The afternoon sunlight fell across the room through the western facing front windows. The floors were wooden and in need of repair. A colorfully drawn map on the wall was circled by photographs of men posing outside a tunnel. The words 'Gruff Station Engineers 1870' were inscribed on the frames. There were two small prison cells. One was occupied by a sleeping man, probably drunk. There was a small desk for one deputy and a larger desk for Sheriff Wayne Mulligan. Two chairs for guests. A potbelly stove with a kettle. Behind the sheriff's desk hung a portrait of President Grant and a framed needlepoint of the Ten Commandments. Sandwiched between these two objets d'art was a secured gun case. The smell of beer tinged sweat and full chamber pots hung like a cloud in the room.

To say Sheriff Wayne Mulligan was large would be straining the word. Pinkerton could scarcely guess how he manage to squeeze himself behind his desk much less actively enforce the law.

Pinkerton pulled out his wallet and showed his badge. "Agent Allan Pinkerton. My associate, Agent Lothar Sigerson."

Mulligan gestured to the chairs.

"No, thank you. This isn't a social call, Sheriff Mulligan. You received my telegraph?"

"Yes. Yes, I did." Mulligan shrugged and waved his beefy hands in the air. "I can't help you."

"Is that so?"

"Your telegraph said you were looking for the content of a wagon that came through here. Lots of wagons come through here." Mulligan shifted his hulk, looked up at the two agents. "Now unless someone does something illegal, I don't get involved. I could be more help if you boys could tell me exactly what you are looking for?"

Sigerson saw the tendons in Pinkerton's jaw twitch so he stepped forward. "That information is classified."

"Then it's all the same to me. I simply can't help you."

"Then I'll make this as simple as I can." Pinkerton pulled three photographs out of his jacket pocket and threw them on the desk. "These men came through this town two weeks ago. One of them, Jonas Samples, sent a telegram to his wife telling her that they were leaving Gruff Springs and heading towards the mountains, and then on to Mexico. According to my sources, they didn't make it to Mexico. Now, I don't give a rat's ass about these men but the cargo they were carrying, I want. The President has empowered me to do whatever it takes to retrieve it."

"THE PRESIDENT?!" The drunk man rolled off his cot and stumbled over to the bars, grabbing them. "The President! He got my telegram about the monsters! See? Sheriff? See?!? The President sent someone to get the monsters!!"

"Aw, hell, you woke him up. Deputy Clarkson! CLARKSON!" Mulligan yelled.

A skinny young deputy ran out from the hallway. "Yes, sir?"

"Excuse me a second, boys. Clarkson, you know my rule about drunks. If they are sober enough to stand..."

"They are sober enough to walk out the door." Clarkson sighed and opened the cell door. "Come on, Gibby. Time to go home."

"No!" The drunk pushed his way passed the deputy and staggered over to Pinkerton. "You...you are here...from the President...to help me. Please, help me? Nobody will listen to me. I knew...I knew the President would send someone to kill them. Kill the monsters." He fell down to Pinkerton's feet, groveling. "Please say you will...please please please...."

Pinkerton helped the man to his feet. The poor wretch was tall but so humped over and folded that he looked half his height. The man's brown eyes were sick and desperate. A wave of heartsick compassion flooded through Pinkerton. "I will. Now, go over to the diner and get something to eat."

He pulled out his wallet and gave the man a dollar. "And get a bath. Man was raised up from the dirt. He was not meant to dwell in it."

"Thank you, thank you, thank you!" he bowed repeatedly, tripping over his own feet. "I knew you'd come… I knew it. I've been telling them….telling them! See?!?"

"Yeah, sure, Gibby." Deputy Clarkson took him by the collar and led him out the door. "Keep out of trouble!"

"I am sorry about that. He's a bit of local color," Sheriff Mulligan said. "That was Duane Gibson. He was part of a wagon train that got wiped out by Indians."

"Indians?" asked Sigerson.

"Indians." The sheriff tugged at his ear. "He says monsters but…" He ended the thought in a shrug. "He lost everything he owned."

"Not a pot to piss in," Clarkson laughed.

Mulligan shot the young deputy a look that shot down his joviality; Pinkerton made a mental note of the gesture.

"Gibby made it back to town alive but his mind is gone. Constantly raving about monsters. We try to keep him quiet because he startles the spa visitors but he's harmless. He wanders around town and does odd jobs for money."

"Old Gibby prefers to sleep in the cell. Says he feels safer behind bars." Clarkson shook his head. "Claims he's saving up for a gun so he can go kill the monsters."

"Please tell me no one would be fool enough to sell him a gun," Sigerson said.

"No need to worry about that. He spends every cent on drink. And I can assure you, sir, that includes your dollar." The sheriff leaned back, cruelly testing the wood of his chair. "But, back to your problem. I don't know these men. I'm sorry. I can't help you."

Pinkerton picked up the photographs. "I thank you for your time."

"That's what I'm here for."

"One more question, sheriff." Pinkerton pointed to the map and photographs on the wall.

"There are two trails leading out of town. One that goes around the mountains and one that goes right through. Our stagecoach didn't find such a shortcut."

"That was a bit of wishful thinking, I'm afraid. What you are looking at is the photographic history of our little town. We were called Gruff Station. It wasn't nothing but a spot in the road for settlers to stop, rest and restock. If you look at that map, you'll see that our little town is nestled in a crescent, almost a bowl. It's like we're hugged in tight by a rocky ridge."

"That must make it hard for supplies and travelers to come into town," said Sigerson.

"It doesn't help."

"Gruff Station had a reputation for lawlessness," interjected Pinkerton. "Because of these mountains, it was a favorite hiding spot for highway men who would rob pioneer wagon trains."

"Ah, you know of our past sins?" Sheriff Mulligan nodded and smiled. "Those stories made it all the way to Chicago?"

"It's my job to know."

"All towns have a past, Agent Pinkerton, and I suspect many of those stories you heard are false. Lies spread by those damn fool prospectors, looking for gold. I've had more than a few spend time in my cells, I can tell you. They spread rumors and gave the ridge a name, Sombra Malo. Bad Shadows. You won't find it on a map. They told tales of bad luck up in the hills. How their tools would go missing. People, too. Even had a German come through complaining that the mountain was full of some kind of goblin. Drunk bastards. Still, that didn't stop pioneers from following the Spanish Trail, heading west, towards California or Mexico.

"Then five years ago, Mr. Mooneyham and some enterprising businessmen decided that the town needed a more direct travel route West. Travelers equal revenue, you see. More travelers, more money. They hired a bunch of engineers from up East. The plan was to blow tunnel through the mountain. That's what that map is illustrating, a pipe dream. Instead they found an underground mineral spring. Well, spring isn't really the right word. It is more like a gushing white-water river. Killed three Chinamen when it first busted out. The engineers built a bridge for the workers but in a year's time, the railroad idea was tossed to the side. The engineers had a new idea. If you can't go through, go under. So, they began to find ways to funnel the water. All sorts of aqueducts and mechanics to get the water a mile from there to the baths down at the Elixir Spa Hotel. I don't have the learning to explain it all. We didn't get our railroad but, all in all, it's been a godsend. We're a successful luxury resort now. People come from all around to sample our waters. No need to rob wandering travelers."

"At least not outwardly, anyway," said Pinkerton.

"People get what they pay for." Mulligan chewed off a hangnail and spit it out. "Are you saying you don't you believe in miracles, Agent Pinkerton?"

"I prefer hard truth to soft words."

"I've read about the Gruff Springs Elixir Spa," Sigerson said, rubbing his back. "It is supposed to cure everything from asthma to tuberculosis."

"It does that and more, Agent Sigerson." The sheriff smiled. "I can vouch for their claims. Their hot water treatments do wonders for my back troubles. If you're staying the night, I could pull some strings and get you sorted out."

"That would be much appreciated," Sigerson said, smiling. "Boss?"

A line of white smoke slipped through Pinkerton's thin lips as he turned towards the door.

"Maybe another time, Sheriff Mulligan. Thank you all the same."

Pinkerton went out to the covered porch. It was a small town despite its reputation. There was only one street through the town. There were two hotels: The Gruff Hotel, directly across from where they were standing, and one further down the street that offered the miracle water treatments. There was a diner, a saloon, a general store, a small church, one bank and a building with no frontage sign but the lace curtains and the red stained lantern was enough to promote the services found within.

Nearby he could see the water tower that supplied the locals and, in the shade of it, a public bath house that was shuttered and closed for business.

Strange, mused Pinkerton.

He walked to the hand pump beside the closed bath house, grabbed the handle and gave it several hard thrusts. A strangled groan erupted and then a trickle of rusty water dribbled down.

"A bit dry for a water town," he murmured.

Sigerson caught up to his employer. "Boss, why did you send a telegraph? You said this was classified."

"I wanted to see who would show up. Know your enemy, Sigerson. Now, go over to the Gruff and get us two rooms that face the street."

"What if they're occupied?"

"Empty them. Then go over to the diner. I'll meet you shortly."

"Where are you going, boss?"

"I am going to see a man about a monster."

Chapter Four

The lantern on the table cast a sickly, yellow glow. They met in a windowless back room because that was the sort of place that men like them preferred to do business.

"Pinkertons!" Talley's voice was shrill and he wiped his forehead.

"Oh, not just run of the mill Pinkertons, boys." Sheriff Mulligan adjusted his bulk. "What we got in our town is THE Pinkerton."

"A cop is a cop," said the young gunman, Garret Reynolds, to his friend. "Goes down just like any other man with enough lead. Am I right, Juan?"

Mooneyham slammed his cane on the table. "Don't you two even think it! The last thing we need in our streets is a dead Pinkerton."

"Much less a dead Allan Pinkerton." Mayor Brown smoothed back his hair. "Do you think they know? About the gold?"

"They didn't say as much but," the huge man shrugged. "Why else would they come all the way here? The water? Ha! Not likely."

"I say we wash our hands of the entire, horrible business," said a relieved Mayor Brown. "Live and let live. The gold stays where it is. If Pinkerton and his goon want to risk their lives for it, that's on their heads."

****

Mooneyham rubbed his forehead.

A Pinkerton! In Gruff Springs!

How did this go so wrong?

He cast an angry eye towards the sheriff. A part of him wished he could put all the blame on that fool Mulligan. He was the one who instigated the foolishness.

I saw it for myself. Two boxes full of gold bricks. Easy pickings. Two of them are drunk over at the Watering Hole. The other two of them are sick with typhus, can barely stand. We could ambush them tonight, right down the street.

At least Mooneyham wasn't so blinded by greed to allow the crime to be done in town. Never shit where you live. It was a creed his grandfather had beat into him.

Still, the fact that he allowed it to happen was a sin that fell squarely on his shoulders.

They waited. The sheriff rounded up a posse of young, strong men who'd do whatever they were told. Talley conjured up the cash. Toad did what the buffoon did best. Nothing.

And Lucas Mooneyham, the savior of Gruff Springs, the entrepreneur extraordinaire who took a town that wasn't anything more than a scab in the desert and turned it into a magic oasis, gave his consent.

And like that, the crime was set.

It'll be just like the old days, Mulligan said. *Easy pickings.*

God damn that man.

In the sheriff's defense, Mooneyham countered, it should have been easy pickings. Everything went as planned. The hooligans

Mulligan hired did the job. They stopped the wagon. Four bullets later, they retrieved the wooden boxes.

Or at least that is the story told by the survivors.

****

Talley pounded his boney fist on the table. "No! Gentlemen, hear me out. This town has only a year before the spring water runs dry. Diverting the town's water into the Spa's reserve will only buy us a few more months. The only thing between us and a life of plush retirement are a few godforsaken mountain men."

"Men?" said Garret Reynolds. "I beg to differ, gentlemen. You haven't been out there. I have lost all my men except Juan here trying to get the gold bars your 'mountain men' dragged into that mountain."

****

"We were getting the boxes and then suddenly a swarm of...of something came out of the mountain! It sounded like locusts as they rushed

*over us. And it was just blood....blood
everywhere!"*

Only two men came back, Garret Reynolds
and Juan Rodrigo. Alive but, unfortunately, without
the gold.

There had been trouble before. Engineers
complained that they thought they were being spied
on, tools would go missing. A dog they kept as a
mascot went missing. The only thing ever found
was three of its paws. He wrote it off as sabotage. A
man like Mooneyham always made enemies.

He never imagined it was monsters. Real,
damn, honest to God monsters.

Mooneyham twisted the silver tipped cane in
the palm of his hands. He could feel it roll under
every knobby arthritic knuckle. Goddamn it. He
was 70 years old. He didn't have the time to rebuild
his empire. He needed that gold. He'd be damned if
he died like a dog in the dirt like his father did
panning for gold.

Gold. That goddamn gold. It always came
back to that filthy lucre. So be it. That was the way

of the world. Nothing was going to stop him. Not Pinkerton. Not monsters. It was going to be his or he'd die trying.

Well, truth be told, not him, per se, but someone.

****

"Settle down, Reynolds," said Mulligan.

"You are paid well," said Talley, smiling with crooked teeth. "I wonder how the families of your dead men would feel if they knew how well, eh? And your partner, Juan. How high on the town is your missus living now?"

Reynolds and Juan shuffled uncomfortably but remained silent.

"And we've all been paid well, Talley. But there comes a time we have to decide how much is enough," said Mooneyham, as he jiggled the gold nugget he kept on his watch chain. "And I don't think that time has come."

"So, we're going for the gold?" asked Mayor Brown.

"Oh, yes. We have no choice. We get as many of the bars as we can carry out and then blow the whole thing to Kingdom Come."

"Wait a minute. We? *WE?* Do you hear that, Juan?" Garret barked out a laugh. "You mean me and Juan here, right? We're all that's left, remember? You don't get it. Those *things* won't let us near it. And now you're expecting us to go waltzing in with dynamite and just blow the place up with sticks of sweaty dynamite that ain't been turned in a year. One bad bump and the world is minus one Garret and a Juan. You are out of your goddamn mind. I'm not dying for you or your damn gold."

"We'll double your pay," offered Talley. Garret pursed his lips as he did the math in his head. Mr. Mooneyham sat back and stared at the silver tip of his cane. "What if you took some help with you? Two extra warm bodies."

Garret and Juan exchanged glances. "You mean fodder."

Mooneyham shrugged. "As you wish."

"I know just the men," said Mulligan. "They scavenge for me. I can get them in an hour." Garret nodded at Juan who shrugged. "Fine. But their horses carry the damn dynamite."

"Fair enough," said Mooneyham. "Then, gentlemen, are we agreed?"

Talley and Mulligan nodded. Mayor Brown patted his hair, sighed deeply and said, "Aye."

"Excellent! In three hours, we'll meet, split up the booty and never see hide nor hair of each other or this wretched town ever again."

Chapter Five

To a city boy like Lothar Sigerson, what Gruff Springs called a hotel, he called a boarding house. More crass fellows back in Chicago would have called it a flophouse but Mama Sigerson had raised her boy to be generous and polite.

The pink rosebuds that dotted the wallpaper had faded into dotty blemishes. The white lace curtains were a strange sort of sunburned beige. The foyer was a collection of velvet chairs and wooden pews, a sad clash of brothel and Sunday school. It was a clean house in that the floors were swept and the counters dusted but the air had that sad, clammy smell that many houses have when they are so rotted away from within no amount of scrubbing and whitewash can hide it.

Sigerson took note of the layout. Agent Pinkerton was always telling the younger detectives to create mental maps to sharpen their observation skills. It was a modest house of simple architecture. Two stories. The lower floor had a foyer, reception room, a dining room to the right that he supposed led to a kitchen beyond. To the left there was a closed door. Probably the manager's quarters. A staircase led to the second floor where there were the rooms to let.

The foyer was empty. The baggage was stacked beside the door. Agent Sigerson looked the luggage over, counting to make sure they were all there and…oh no. Oh, no!

He went to the counter that served as a reception desk and picked up a hand bell. CLANG! CLANG! CLANG! The heavy clapper made the bell nearly jump of out his hand.

"Hold horses. I'm coming, I'm coming." An elderly Chinese man came thumping down the stairs. His shoulders stooped as if he was pulling a heavy wagon as he shuffled over to the reception table. He pulled out a ledger and a held out a pen to the Swede towering over him. "Checking in?"

"Yes, but there is a problem."

He pushed the ledger towards him. "Sign."

"Wait, there is a problem. See those bags over there?"

"Yes. Grumpy old man smelled of horse brought them in. Your bags? You want a room? Sign."

"One of them is missing. A very important bag about so big?" Sigerson held his hands roughly four feet apart. "Do you know what happened to it?"

The old man thumped the ledger. "You want a room? Sign."

"No, you don't understand."

"No room?" He swept the ledger book away.

"Take stinky bags and leave."

"No. I do want a room but first I need to find my bag."

The ledger appeared magically back on the countertop. "Room? Sign."

Sigerson remembered his mother's upbringing and counted to five. "Is there a manager?"

"You want manager?"

"Yes. I want manager."

He pushed the ledger towards Sigerson.

"Sign."

"Sign? But why?"

"Only guests get to manager. Sign."

"Fine!" Sigerson signed the ledger book. "Now, the manager. Where is he?"

"The Manager," Sigerson heard a voice that was very much not a him say, "is right behind you. Welcome to the Gruff Hotel."

Sigerson's mouth went dry. She stood in the doorway of the formerly mentioned closed door. Her wavy auburn hair was in a bun held so loosely that ringlets framed her face. She had pale blue eyes, pink lips and a dusting of freckles across her nose that made her seem ageless. She wore a clean, crisp linen blouse that buttoned up to the neck, but he couldn't help notice that the buttoning didn't make it that far. Her gold brocade vest clinched in around her waist and set off the brown of her long skirt. He couldn't see her shoes and instantly imagined her barefoot.

No, the manager was definitely not a man.

"I'm Fran. I run this place. That is Mr. Chin." She walked around him and settled next to the Chinaman. Sigerson was suddenly aware of the smell of tangerines that lingered where she passed. He smoothed out his wrinkled shirt, suddenly very self-conscious of how he looked after a hard day's ride. "I saw you earlier today. You came in with that man with the pipe. The one that made Old Mooneyham nearly drop a brick."

The Chinaman sniggered. "Heh. Brick."

"Sorry?"

"The one with the shiny mail ordered stick. Mooneyham owns most of the town. Bought everything up when they tapped that damned spring. Anyone that can make that old snake shake in his boots is a friend in my book."

"Heh. Snake."

She used a long finger to trace down the ledger. "Lothar?"

"Ah, yes. My name is Lothar Sigerson. Agent Sigerson," he said, showing off his badge.

"I need to get two rooms. One for me and one for my partn-" He stopped himself. No one called themselves Allan Pinkerton's partner. They were his associates, employees of the National Pinkerton Detective Agency. Never his partner. "My boss."

"Pinkertons, huh? Well, I hope you gents aren't the discriminating type, Agent Sigerson. "

"Pardon?"

"Most people that come through this town are city people here for the miracle cures down the street at the Elixir Spa. Like they say in town, 'you only stay in the Gruff if you like it rough'." Sigerson made an effort to keep his jaw from dropping. *Focus, Lothar, focus. There was something else. Something important.* "Missing luggage!"

"Excuse me?"

"The luggage over there. It's ours and there is one missing. A very important piece about so big? It was in a special gun case."

"Oh, yes. The gun. I put it in the safe in my room. We don't allow guests to have guns in the rooms. It leads to trouble."

"Fine. I understand but this is very valuable. The only one of its kind, really."

"Really? Perhaps you could show it to me?" She leaned over the counter and her buttons strained against her vest. "I've seen my share of Colts and Winchesters. It'll be a treat to see something different."

Sigerson counted to five and released his breath slowly. "Fine but first, I need rooms. We'd like them facing the street, if they are available."

"No problem. Chin? Take the luggage upstairs and clear out the two front rooms."

"McCormick brothers are in the front rooms. How?"

"Toss a bottle of whiskey out the window and tell the drunk bastards they can fly for all I care. Just do it."

"Heh. Fly." He gathered up the heavy duffel bags on his already bent back and began climbing the stairs.

"Chin might be awhile. He's good help but a little slow." She closed the ledger book and slid it under the counter. She crossed over to the Swede and took his arm. "Now, come with me and show me this one of kind gun you claim to have."

Chapter Six

Main Street ran into two different worlds.

To the east, towards mountain ridge, where the aqueducts ran into the Gruff Miracle Elixir baths, the street was full of city people in fancy clothes, taking in the evening air before settling down for the night with a bedtime mineral water enema.

Allan Pinkerton chewed on the stem of his pipe as he slowly walked past the smiling tourists. Colorful banners hung from every storefront and balcony, "DRINK GRUFF ELIXIR!" and "THE WATER IS THE LIFE!" preached in ten-inch letters on white canvas cloth that flapped in the evening breeze. In one window, a billboard advertisement told the story of ANCIENT PEOPLES that wandered THESE LANDS who drank from the MAGICAL WATER. There was an illustration of sickly old man with a limp feather headdress and woman dressed in a burlap sack entering into a pool and then exiting young and beautiful, her burlap sack miraculously transformed into a beautiful dress and his feathers starched and stiff. 'INDIAN PRINCESSES swam in the ELIXIR to become BEAUTIFUL! INDIAN BRAVES drank the ELIXIR to be BRAVE and VIRILE!'

Pinkerton smirked. Whiskey was the only elixir he knew that made weak men brave and homely women beautiful. Still, the businessman in him appreciated the science behind the marketing. People will believe anything if you show it to them in pictures.

The people in the town seemed sincere enough. Some were here for the curiosity of the latest health fad. What harm could a dip in a hot bath do? Besides, if it put the starch in some feathers, who was harmed? There were the others, the phlegmatic consumptives desperate for a miracle that gave Pinkerton pause to wonder if there were something sinful in giving the desperate such false hope.

Towards the west, the street grew grayer and emptier. Only a few hardier souls ventured this far away from the spa circle. Pinkerton chose to turn and walk towards that side of town. He just felt more at home.

He clamped down on the pipe and puffed out a small cloud. Perhaps there was something criminal in selling magic water to the dying but that wasn't the crime he was here to investigate. He couldn't allow himself to get distracted. He had to keep focused on the case at hand: the Confederate gold earmarked for mercenaries in Mexico.

Nearly ten years after the war and some diehards were still fighting the Lost Cause. Pinkerton was able to intercept a telegram sent from Gruff Springs that they were 'heading into the mountains'. *Into the mountains.* The two paths on the map in the sheriff's office. 'Entire group was wiped out by Indians.' *Indians.* Pinkerton puffed his pipe at the audacity of the deceit. As if he'd be fool enough to believe such a lie. It was so easy to shift the blame onto a boogey man when lying to the uninformed.

Indians.

Monsters.

Pinkerton quickened his pace and crossed the street towards the Watering Hole saloon.

****

The Watering Hole catered mainly to the locals. If you wanted velvet and soft chairs, you'd have to go the other direction, down towards the Elixir Hotel and Spa. Alan Pinkerton took a quick critical glance. One door to the street. A bar that ran the length of the wall with two doors on either side, probably leading to rooms behind. A staircase to the left led to rooms for rent. There were three tables in the middle of the room and six others to the side, pushed against the wall, hidden in shadows. One bartender, a big man stood behind the bar with his beefy arms crossed, nodded at Pinkerton, a quick signal: *I see you.* Alan returned to gesture. *I see you, too.* Eight men sitting at tables. Three playing cards. The atmosphere was peaceable. The air smelled of sweat, spilled beer with an underlying aura of tobacco smoke.

Duane Gibson wasn't a hard man to find. Give a drunk a dollar and it is as good as having him on a leash. The man who saw monsters was drinking alone, with his back to the door, spreading out his few remaining coins on the table. Pinkerton shook his head. *Idiot.*

"Mr. Gibson?"

The man flinched. Pinkerton moved in front of him and held out his hand. Gibson swept his coins off the table. He looked up with blank, runny eyes. "I was only countin' up what I got left. I only got one…just one drink and I'm going to save the rest."

"I'm Agent Pinkerton. We met before at the sheriff's office. Do you remember me?" Pinkerton smiled; a rare treat for anyone to see. "I need to ask you some questions about the monsters."

"I remember. Yes…I remember." Gibson raised the glass up to his lips with a shaky hand and finished off the whiskey. "I remember lots of things."

Pinkerton sat down across from Gibson, facing the door. "What do you remember?"

"I got nearly three dollars saved up." He smiled, his teeth like small black tombstones. "Butch," Gibson nodded towards the bartender, "says he can get me a good gun for a few dollars more. That's what he always says. Every time I come in here and show him what I got, he just says, 'Just a few dollars more, Duane.' It's always just....just that much out of my reach. But one day...one day, I'll have enough and then, there will be a reckoning. You just watch me. I'll have one of them monster's heads stuffed and mounted over that fireplace. You just watch and see! Then people won't laugh at me."

Pinkerton wished he'd brought Sigerson. His agent was good with people. He was built like a bear and twice as strong but Sigerson was patient as a lamb. The exact opposite of his boss who had the patience of a badger with a toothache. Pinkerton took a deep breath and kept smiling. Sigerson was always smiled. Perhaps that was the trick. "Mr. Gibson. Tell me about the monsters."

"Tell you? Sure…sure." Gibson licked his lips and flicked a look at his empty whiskey glass. Ah, bribery. This made Pinkerton happy. He knew where he stood with a bribe. He snapped his fingers and motioned for Butch to bring them some whiskey. "Leave the bottle. I understand how thirsty a man can get talking."

Gibson held up his glass in salute and took a sip. "There was three of us. Three wagons. All of us headed towards California. Aiming for it, anyway. Me and my Elsie would've settled for anywhere after being on the trail for so long. Travel never suited my Elsie. She was sickly. Thought maybe the climate out West would suit her more. Hah, little did we know." He shakily took another sip. "We stopped in Gruff Station for supplies. This was just a stop over town back then. Nobody stayed for long. Not much in the way of, well, anything. I remember this town when it was a gangly gray goose, before it turned into a fancy town swan. Well," he waved his hand around the bar, "some of the town, anyway."

Patience, patience. "You were going to California?"

"Yes, California. We took the trail that the fellow told us about."

"Who told you to go that way?"

"A fancy fellow with blonde hair they called Toad gave us directions. Said it was a shortcut. It sure as hell didn't look like no shortcut but we trusted him."

Interesting. "I see, please, continue."

"It was late afternoon by that time and my Elsie…she wasn't feeling very well. So, we decided to set up camp. What was one more day? Just one more day cut out of a long tapestry of days. Where was the harm? Where?"

"Mr. Gibson." Pinkerton splashed more whiskey into the glass. "The monsters?'

"Ain't that something? Nobody else wants to hear me talk about the monsters. And here you come, out of nowhere and want me to talk about nothing but!" Gibson took a sloppy sip. "Ain't that something new?"

Pinkerton felt his face begin to hurt under the strain of pleasantly smiling. "Well, it's all a part of the job, Mr. Gibson, know your enemy."

"Hooohaw! Listen to him talk. Know your enemy. Listen to me, Mr. Pinkerton. There ain't nothing more than you need to know than this fact," he thumped the table with his finger, "there are monsters out there! Monsters that come out of the dark. They rip, tear, and kill! Monsters straight from hell!"

"And it is my duty to stop them." Pinkerton lips straightened back into their natural razor edge. "Continue."

Gibson looked away and concentrated on running a dirty fingernail along a scratch in the tabletop. "We camped…"

"You established that. Did you make a campfire?"

"What…yes, of course. Elsie had to make dinner. We needed the fire to keep warm and keep away animals."

And to make your presence known to anyone in the area. "Continue."

Gibson tipped his empty glass. "Maybe a little more."

"After you tell me more. Continue. When did they…the monsters attack?"

"Sunset. The only light to see by was from the fire and from the lanterns we kept lit."

"What did they look like?"

Gibson's tongue clicked on the roof of his dry mouth. "My throat is parched from talking. Maybe just one more before I continue…"

"Details, Mr. Gibson. What did they look like?"

"I don't know!" Gibson screamed, spraying spittle as he cried out. He pulled at his greasy hair and began to sob. "We didn't see them…not at first. No, but we could hear them. It was a loud clickety-clickety-clickety chorus, like cicadas in the summer.

Ever heard them? Do they have them in big fancy towns like Chicago? They can make the air vibrate with their clickety clickety clickety songs."

Fireworks and clappers coming at them from the darkness, more like. Pinkerton rubbed his chin. *Horses with chains or something jingly as to disorient the victims.*

"Then what happened?"

"Randall Kohl, he was our leader, told the women folk to take cover in a wagon. He had all sorts of military bearing. I heard he fought in the Indian wars."

Pinkerton nodded. "Continue."

"Then we got our guns and lanterns and went looking for what was making the sound. Mainly to comfort the women, at first. Randall was lead, next was Donnie and then Gunther. I brought up the rear. I stayed behind, for just a minute or two. To make sure the women were safe."

"Of course. Continue."

"I was just coming up and I could hear Randall call out, "Who's there?" and the sound….the clickety-click… it *turned*... focused on him. I can't describe it any better. He took another step closer and held up his lantern. I finally caught up with Gunther, who was slow because of a wooden leg, when Randall screamed a blasphemy I won't repeat and he just started shooting. Randall ran at us, screaming to run, runrunrunrun! Run back to the wagons! We did just that. I had never been so scared. And I weren't alone. I remember Gunther keeping up, step for step, with us, wooden leg be damned. We all knew that if it was something that could scare Randall, it was something to hightail it from but quick."

"What did Randall see?'

"I'll tell you what he told me, Mr. Pinkerton, when we got back to camp. He went straight to loading weapons, not even stopping to check on his woman, and I asked him, 'Good Lord, Randall. What's out there? What's got you so shook up?' and he looked me right in the eyes, the same way I am looking straight at you and he said, 'Duane, I looked into maw of a demon."

"A demon? You call them monsters."

"That's were his words. Randall had more of a Bible bent to him, always quoting scripture, giving me the eye when I'd take a nip from my flask. Now, I don't mean to speak ill of the dead but, he did sometimes rub me raw."

"Gibson, what did *you* see?"

Gibson licked his cracked lips. "Sure I can't have a drop of that drink?"

Pinkerton shook his head.

"I'm going to need it if want me to revisit hell."

Pinkerton poured two fingers into the glass. "Continue."

Gibson slammed the amber liquid into his gullet and turned the glass over onto the table. "No more. Not until I finish. But when I do, I want the rest of that bottle to myself. Agreed?"

Pinkerton nodded.

Gibson took a deep breath, his chest expanding so that he sat up straight. He let the breath go and he sagged but only slightly. "I remember the horses screaming. All five of them, screaming like a chorus. Randall took Donnie with him. He told me and Gunther to stay behind. 'Give the women weapons.' he said before running off. Gunther did as he was told. I stood there. I remember watching their shapes disappearing into the night until only the light of their lanterns broke through the dark. I heard Randall shout something and they started shooting. I remember bringing my own rifle up, out of reflex more than anything useful. I just stood there. Waiting, just waiting. So damn useless. While Randall and Donnie were out there, dying.

"The women had grabbed what they had. Randall's wife was pregnant and stayed in the wagon. Donnie's girls, Lizzie and Deirdre, had a Colt each. They were his pride and joy. Red curly hair just like their daddy. He was always teaching his daughters how to take care of themselves, shooting at prairie dogs. They were good shots. They provided us more dinners than I can count. Gunther's wife, Mona, had a long plank of wood. I remember she used it for laundry whenever we had the chance for such a luxury. Boiling water, cleaning our underwear. She was mad about cleanliness. And my Elsie. Poor Elsie had found my Bowie knife. I turned to see them standing by the campfire, their jaws set to fight but terror, mad fear, glistened in their eyes.

"We never stood a chance in hell, Mr. Pinkerton. Believe me when I tell you that if we had all the ammunition of the Union Army behind us, it wouldn't have done any good against the hellions that swarmed over us that night!"

"*What*?" Pinkerton gritted his teeth. "What did you see?!"

"Monsters! Like I've been saying for the past fifteen years! Goddamn monsters! Ain't no other name for them. In the light of the campfire, I could see them, but I don't know how to rightly describe them. Gray, mottled skin. As if no sunlight had ever kissed it. Huge eyes like dinner plates. Pugged nose squished back to the brow and a mouth that looked too big for its head. Full of teeth. Fierce, snapping teeth. They grabbed at us with long spindly arms that ended in needle sharp claws. They scuttled like roaches coming out from under the bridge, out from the tunnel, over the rocks, hell, out from under the ground for all I could tell. In minutes, dozens of them flooded over us.

"We fought back, little good it did us. They took bullets as if their skin was made of cheese. Water spurted out, not blood! Water! And the skin just clogged back over like clay. Mona had more luck with the wood. She swung and decapitated three before she lost her footing and they fell in on her. I never saw what happened to Donnie's girls. My Elsie. My beautiful Elsie. She fought. I can't tell you how proud I was of her. She gave them hell, slicing and swiping at those bastards with that heavy Bowie knife. She took one of the monster's arm right off at the elbow! I remember how that damned thing screamed, how the scream seemed to roll through the sky, like thunder.

"It just called more of them over to where my Elsie stood. I tried to run over to her but…I…tripped. I fell to my knees. The last thing I saw was my Elsie being held down, her eyes locked onto me, as her hair, her long beautiful blonde hair was scalped off."

A scalping? Interesting. A way to lead the curious to believe that Indians were culpable.

"I don't remember anything else. Days later, I woke up in a cell." Gibson turned his glass over. "I'll take that drink now."

Pinkerton poured and slid the bottle over to Gibson. He shot down the whiskey, poured another, drank it, tossed the glass and gulped from the bottle as if trying to burn away the words that had come from his throat.

"Thank you, Mr. Gibson," Agent Pinkerton said. He stood and nodded his head towards the poor drunk. "You've been most helpful."

"Promise me one thing, Mr. Pinkerton. Promise me you'll kill them, kill them all. Not for me. I'm not worth skinning. I'm shit. Kill them for my poor Elsie."

"I will do my duty." Allan Pinkerton tipped his bowler hat. "That you can be sure."

<u>Chapter Seven</u>

The rooms were small, the wallpaper was more paste than paper, and the beds were hard but the windows faced the street. Agent Sigerson looked out the window, down at the sheriff's office below. Four men were leaving, or, to be more accurate, four heavily armed men were leaving, walking very quickly towards the end of the walk, turning left to where they kept the stables. He made a mental note to tell Pinkerton about them at dinner. Speaking of, Sigerson checked his pocket watch and cursed the time. His little distraction downstairs cost him an hour and change but it was worth it.

Agent Sigerson's back wasn't hurting anymore.

On a plain wooden table next to the nicked up mirrored chest of drawers, there was an ornate pitcher sitting in a matching wash basin. It was a thing of beauty, like something you'd seen in a fine home on the East Coast. The handle was carved like a green stem to match the rose lipped spout. Chin had filled it with cool, clean water and Sigerson lost all interest in how such a feminine thing came to be in such a dirty place as he poured the water in the basin. He cupped his hands and splashed the water on his face.

Lord, have mercy. It was the simple things, truly, to give thanks for…

The door slammed open. Sigerson sputtered in surprise.

"Get your things," Pinkerton said, grabbing a towel and throwing it at him. "We're going to the mountain."

"Sure, Boss, but what about dinner?"

"Mine was delicious. Be downstairs in ten minutes." He took a quick glance around the room. "Where is Thor?"

"Fran has it in her room."

Pinkerton raised an eyebrow and shook his head. "Bring it. Ten minutes." And left.

Sigerson wiped his face and threw the towel over the basin, never noticing the delicate engraving of golden letters glittering through the water. *For my beautiful Elsie.*

Chapter Eight

Agent Sigerson met Pinkerton outside the Gruff Hotel with two horses already saddled and ready to go.

"You have Thor?"

Sigerson nodded and held up his gun case. Inside was a modified percussion cap, muzzle loaded seven-barreled Nock gun. Only five hundred were made for the Royal Navy but after scores of broken shoulders from the recoil of seven barrels firing at once, the gun was recalled. The Royal Navy considered the gun too hard to aim and control for an average man, but they didn't take into consideration someone like Lothar Sigerson. Not only was he not intimidated by a gun, he was a man who liked to tinker, to adapt things to his liking. He focused the power of the projectile and dampened the recoil. He also found a way around the nasty problem of flying sparks that had a reputation of burning down the riggings of ships. Lothar Sigerson had, in his spare time, tamed the Nock and renamed it Thor, in honor of his Norwegian heritage.

"The man at the stables said it's only an hour or so ride towards the mountains."

"I saw four men from the sheriff's office head out that way, Boss."

"So, they have a half an hour lead or more." Pinkerton squinted at the sun and then checked his pocket watch. There was only a few more hours until sunset. "Oh, I almost forgot." He pulled a balled napkin out of his coat pocket and threw it down to Sigerson. "Courtesy of the landlady."

Sigerson opened the napkin and found two biscuits, one ham and one honey.

"Seems you made an impression," said Pinkerton.

"Apparently, not enough to get one with jelly."

"Oh, you did. It was delicious."

Chapter Nine

Sigerson finished off the ham biscuit and pocketed the one with honey for later while Pinkerton grimly smoked his pipe. The thin, reedy smelling smoke trailed behind him as he quickly relayed his conversation with Duane Gibson.

"He's a drunk, sir. Can he be trusted?"

"His memories are false but replace his idea of monsters with men dressed as Indians and the story falls into place. I suspect the men we saw leaving tonight are in league with whoever robbed Gibson's wagon and God only knows what else. This isn't just about lost Confederate gold anymore, Sigerson. We've stumbled on a nest of highwaymen, luring and robbing wagon trains and killing settlers. They hit the motherlode when they ran across our men with the Confederate gold."

"But why? The town is booming since the discovery of the spring water."

"Gruff Station was a notorious town before it softened into Gruff Springs. Sometimes old ways are hard to break. Are you familiar with the story of Sawney Bean?"

"No, sir. Should I be?"

"He's a Scottish boogeyman." Pinkerton leaned back into his saddle. "Story goes that back in the 15th century, Sawney Bean and his family of twenty or so miscreants traveled the highways robbing, killing and eating anyone they came across. This case, I fear, has a bit of a Bean flavor to it."

"I still don't understand why-"

Just then, the staccato rapping of gunshots ripped through the air.

The screaming followed.

"Hold that thought and follow me," Pinkerton said as he kicked his horse into a full run.

Chapter Ten

A thundering cloud came at them. Three horses, crazed and frothy with fear, galloped at full force, driving a wedge between Pinkerton and Sigerson. The dust kicked up by their frantic hooves choked both men, blinding them. Coughing, Pinkerton pulled tightly on the reins, causing his horse to whinny and turn away. Sigerson called out to his ride, squeezing its sides forcefully with his knees as he tried to contain the frightened beast.

Sigerson pulled his shirt up over his mouth to keep from gagging. "What the hell, boss?"

Pinkerton swiped at the dirty air with his bowler until he could see. "There! Look, there!"

Ahead of them about fifty feet away were four men. One man was crouched behind a dead horse while another man fired his gun, laying cover as he tried to help his friend. Two other men were firing wildly into at a pack of…a pack of…*things*. They were swarming on the men, crab crawling towards the men like a pale gray wave, chittering and chattering as they poured out of the hole in the mountainside. Whatever they were, the bullets the men pumped into them did nothing to push them back.

"Those men are doomed," said Sigerson.

"And with them dies the information I need." Pinkerton pulled out his Colt .45. "Ride!" he commanded as he and Sigerson barreled into the fray.

Chapter Eleven

His gun made a hollow click sound.

"Damn!" Enoch threw the worthless piece of metal at the critter, thunking it in the head. "Ha! Eat that, you son of a bitch!"

He ran towards his brother, Larry, who was hunkered down behind a dead horse. He looked over his shoulder at the other two, Garret and Juan, standing their ground and…no, wait….strike that. He saw them go down as the critters swarmed them, throwing bits and parts of them in the air.

"Shit," he breathed the word more than spoke it as he jumped over the horse and landed beside Larry.

"Enoch!"

"Shit…your arm is all busted up."

"Son of a bitch clawed me good."

He pulled off his shirt and tore off a strip. "Keep down! I gotta get this bandage on tight."

"Wait. What's that?"

Enoch peeked over the brown crest of the horse to see two men on horseback ride up. The one in the bowler hat shot into the gray swarm with a .45. *Dumbass.* Then he said something to the big guy who got off his horse, pulled out a rifle and....

Booooom!

"What the hell is that?!?!" said Larry.

"As far as I'm concerned, that is my new best friend!"

Chapter Twelve

Pinkerton took his hands off his ears as the echoes from Thor died down. The creatures ran screeching and skittering back to the bridge, melting into the darkness of the tunnel. There were a few, slower and smaller that lingered around the bodies, hurriedly picking off meat the bigger ones had left behind. Pinkerton got off his horse, aimed his Colt and shot one square in the forehead. It fell over dead. The few remaining ran to the cover of the bridge. A crippled one, with a stump for an arm, stayed behind and made a move to cannibalize its fallen brethren. "You son of a bitch," Pinkerton snarled and shot at it. The bullet pierced through its shoulder and water squirted out from the wound. It raised its stump of an arm at Pinkerton, hissed and hobbled back to the bridge.

"Well, I'll be damned." Pinkerton looked at the remains of the two men and shook his head. He squatted beside the body of the…he hated to even think the word….*the monster*. It was about four feet tall. The skin had the color and texture of curdled milk. It stank of moss and damp. The feet were flat. The hands curved into talons with four claws. The bald head was squashed down on its shoulder, no neck to speak of. The face was flat, pugged, with only slits for nostrils. The mouth was too big and full of teeth. The eyes were open and looking up in surprise at the bullet hole in the middle of its forehead. "Gibson." Pinkerton stood up. "You poor bastard."

"Boss. Over here. Got some survivors."

"Excellent. Agent Sigerson, reload Thor and stand watch while I introduce myself."

Sigerson nodded and went to work.

He put one foot up on the flank of the dead horse and looked down on the two men. They were both ginger haired, lumpy headed men, poorly dressed in torn shirts and dirty dungarees. At least they were sober. Pinkerton filed both men under the label, 'lackey'.

"I'm Allan Pinkerton of the Pinkerton National Detective Agency. You've probably heard of me." He pulled out his pipe, tapped the bowl clear and packed it with fresh tobacco. "Well, lads, I suspect you have a story to tell."

Chapter Thirteen

Sigerson hoisted Thor on his shoulder and kicked the dead creature's body. It rolled over and moldy water poured out of the hole in its forehead. He felt a shudder of revulsion. The thing was something out of a nightmare- no, more specifically, something out of a fairy tale.

"I've seen this thing before."

He stood over the thing's body and was overwhelmed by a sense of nostalgia and déjà vu. The smells from his mother's kitchen filled his head. Fish, potatoes and heavy cream. Bread, hot and fresh from the oven. She would pull off a piece and feed young Lothar as he sat on her lap and read to him from a book she brought with her from Sweden. It was as large as her lap and filled with colorful, terrifying and beautiful pictures.

"This is the story of a young boy," she read, *"a strong, handsome son that always did as he was told. One day, as he was taking a cow to market, he had to cross over a bridge that he knew was*

troubled by horrible, ugly creatures with pig snouts that snorted and sniffed out humans and sharp teeth to tear flesh off bones.

"Trolls.

"As he and the cow crossed over the bridge, the ugly troll crawled out from underneath and stopped the boy. 'This is my bridge and you must pay the toll!"

"The boy was brave and stood his ground, 'What is the toll?'

"The troll was confused," his mother said. "Normally, people would run away, and the troll would go after them, and eat them. But this brave boy was different. He stood still and did not run. And then the troll had something few trolls ever did. He had an idea. "Maybe I could get some gold, a cow, as well as the flesh of a tender boy."

"The troll's terrible toothy maw broke open in a smile and it said, 'Three, no, four, NO! Six gold coins and I will let you go free.'

'Oh, is that all? This is a fine bridge. I thought you'd charge more.'

'Oh?" The greedy troll rubbed his craggy chin. "You think so?'

'Oh, yes! My big brother who is coming after me will give you sixteen gold coins.' The boy lied. 'He much fatter than skinny, little me and he has three cows.'

'Bigger than you?' The troll stared at the boy. He was a scrawny thing now that it looked at him. 'And three cows?'

'Three fat cows. Much bigger than mine, I am ashamed to say.'

'Feh!' The troll waved him across. 'Go! I will wait for your brother.'

'Good morrow!' said the boy said and went on his way, leaving the Troll to wait forever and ever for a brother that would never come for trolls were as stupid as they were ugly.

Those watercolor prints from his mother's fairytale books were the meat of all his childhood nightmares. When he grew up, he put all those monsters away, assured that such things could not exist outside the book's pages.

But here it was, wetting the toes of his boots.

"I know you," he whispered to confirm it to himself. "I do."

Sigerson hoped Pinkerton was open minded enough to listen

Chapter Fourteen

"So, tell me, boys," said Pinkerton, chewing on his pipe. "What are you all doing out here?"

"We, me and Larry here, we come out here every couple of days and…and-"

"Salvage," offered Larry.

"Yeah, that's the word. Salvage stuff we can find. People leave stuff behind, all the time."

"All the time."

"Let me make myself clearer, boys. Did the Sheriff and his friends hire you boys to come out here for anything special?" asked Pinkerton. "Gold brick bars. About so big? Probably told you they were hidden in the mountain?"

The two men shrugged.

"Is that how you're going to play this, boys? Because I could easily enough just leave you both here to *salvage* all alone against whatever godforsaken horrors are lurking out there in the rocks. Would you like that?"

They shook their heads, their eyes large as saucers.

"Good, then tell me. The gold. Where is it?"

"To hell with it," Larry spat on the ground, holding his bleeding arm. "I don't know anything about some damn gold. We were paid to lay down some dynamite and blow up the tunnel."

"Dynamite? Why would they want to blow up their cash cow?"

"I don't know but it's true," said Enoch. "I swear. We weren't told nothing other than to lay down some sticks. Mulligan hires us sometimes to do odd jobs. My brother, Larry, dabbles in explosives."

"Who were those two?"

"Those two other fellas, Garret and Juan, they were the guys in charge," said Larry. "They went inside the tunnel and then they came running out with those damn things on their heels."

"Hand to God, sir! We don't know anything else."

Just then, Sigerson ran up to Pinkerton.

"Boss, I think I know what these things are."

"Explain."

"My mother had a book of folktales from her village in Sweden. She used to tell me if I were bad, the Trold would come and eat me. Those things look exactly like the monsters in the book."

"Trold?"

"Trolls. Imagine a Swedish version of your Sawney Bean. They live in craggy places, mountains, under bridges. Thieves and hoarders, they steal whatever they want and-"

"Eat whoever crosses over their bridge. I'm familiar with the Grimm version, yes. How do we kill them?"

Sigerson was shaken for a moment at how readily his boss had taken to the idea. "Well, I don't know. The stories were more about tricking them, not killing them. But shooting them in the head seems to work."

"We don't have the ammunition to take on a hundred of them," Pinkerton huffed. "So what are they afraid of? In the stories?"

Sigerson tapped Thor against his leg. "I remember something about storms. Lightning....no, thunder. They hated thunder. Something about a fight with the old gods."

Pinkerton look at the mouth of the tunnel. He inhaled from his pipe and let the smoke roll out of his mouth. *So, thunder, is it? How many are in there?* He clenched down on the stem of his pipe.

"Sigerson. Fetch my binoculars from my saddlebag."

"Sure thing, boss."

Sigerson handed the brass binoculars to Pinkerton. There was still an hour left of sunlight and he explored the tunnel at a comfortable and safe space.

Extended from the mouth of the tunnel was a long, large pipe that funneled the water into a man-made lake from which the water then was channeled into more pipes that led to the Elixir

Springs Hotel. The whole project looked shaky and not built to last. Pinkerton grumbled. More proof that Gruff Springs was full of shysters.

He looked back to the cave and examined the bridge. It was rotting away. Beyond it, an ethereal golden sheen glowed. Pinkerton furrowed his brow. *Could that be the gold? Odd. Why is it shining like that?*

Propped in the wood of the bridge and into the crags around the opening were sticks of dynamite. Sweaty, weeping dynamite. He followed the wire to the detonator lying near the bodies of the other men.

"Sigerson, I have an idea but we'll need help." He pointed at Enoch and Larry. "Have you two ever been officially deputized?"

"No, sir," they chorused.

"You are now, lads. Welcome to the Pinkertons. Give these boys badges Agent."

Sigerson dipped into his front pocket, pulled out two tin stars and gave them to the men

"You always carry badges with you?" asked Larry.

"You're not the first deputized on the spot."

"Hey," said Enoch. "Why is mine all bent up?"

"Like I said. You're not the first."

<u>Chapter Fifteen</u>

Larry and Enoch's first duties as deputies were to build a fire and stand watch. So far, this new job wasn't much different from the old one: shut up and do what you're told. The best thing was taking potshots at the critters that kept popping out from under the bridge. It helped the time go by. Enoch took aim with the Winchester at a fat one that crawled alongside the outer wall. He chipped the stone and the critter scurried back into the dark.

"You missed."

"Go to hell, Larry."

Their new bosses squatted a little further away, lanterns making their shadows dance as they carved in the dirt with knives. They were planning something that the bigger man wasn't happy about. He argued but Pinkerton just jutted out his jaw and stared him down until he finally conceded, and the planning went on.

Larry sat by the fire, fiddling with the bandages on his left arm. "What do you think they're doing over there?"

Enoch raised the rifle and took aim again. "Probably working on getting us killed."

No sooner than the bullet left the rifle, Pinkerton was standing over the pair.

"Listen up, lads. The plan is simple. Agent Sigerson and will stand by the plunger. You two will go west and create a diversion. That will attract the trolls, so I can sneak inside their stronghold, collect the cache of gold, and, when I come back and give the signal, Agent Sigerson will blow the place to hell."

The two men stared at Pinkerton blankly.

"Is he serious?" asked Enoch.

Sigerson nodded, his face pale. "He is always serious."

"Well, color me wrong, Larry. It looks like he was planning on getting himself killed!"

Chapter Sixteen

"Let's calibrate our pocket watches, Agent," he said and Sigerson complied. "Good. Make sure you keep your eye on the time. Thirty minutes."

Sigerson nodded. "Thirty minutes."

Pinkerton took off his coat and hat. Stripping down to his undershirt and pants, he felt naked. He gave his Colt to Larry. The only things he took with him were his timepiece, a small gas lamp, a Bowie knife and a haversack to carry the gold.

"Sir, keep the pistol," Sigerson said. "Please."

"No. The noise would give me away."

"Sir, I insist."

Pinkerton slapped him on the arm. "Just be ready on that plunger."

"I hate to even speculate on this, sir, but, what if you don't make it back in thirty minutes?"

"If I'm not back by then," Pinkerton stroked his beard and gave one of his very rare smiles.

"Odds are there won't be much of me left *to* come back out. Do your duty, Agent. Blow that godforsaken hole to hell."

Chapter Seventeen

The boys were out of sight of their new employers, but they were definitely not alone.

The chittering shadows followed them. Gray bulbous heads popped up behind the rocks, keeping tabs on the wandering men. They were a tempting target but Sigerson had told them to save their ammunition.

"I hope you have a plan," said Enoch as he adjusted his Winchester.

"Actually, I do." Larry pulled out a handful of silver sticks from his haversack. He handed a bunch to Enoch and kept the rest for himself.

"Sparklers?"

"Why not? They like shiny things."

Larry struck a match and lit the stick. A brief crackle and sharp, fiery sparkles zig zagged in the dark. He threw the stick far to the left of them and the shadows chased it like dogs after a ball.

"That's brilliant!" said Enoch.

"It buys us a few minutes at least," said Larry.

Suddenly, there was a screech as the light was snuffed out.

"Until they squash it out. Some dumbasses never learn," he said as he lit another one.

"The same can be said for a lot of people, I hear," said a voice from behind them.

Larry turned to face the speaker. It was Lucas Mooneyham on horseback. Beside him also on horseback were Edmund Talley and Mayor Brown. Sheriff Mulligan was bringing up the rear, holding the rein of a very tired horse.

Mulligan pulled a Winchester from the holster attached to his saddle. The other three men also revealed their firearms.

Chapter Eighteen

Pinkerton turned up his lamplight and the darkness in the tunnel melted away to reveal the craggy walls that arched around him. The air was dank, cool and had a strange tinge of rot. He moved forward, carefully keeping balance on the rickety wooden bridge that abruptly ended ten feet ahead of him.

He checked his pocket watch. Six minutes had passed. He took a deep breath, grimacing at the putrid meat smell. A soft wind that reeked of decay tickled his cheek. To the left, there was a four-foot high, three-foot-wide crack. The glow peeked out of it like shy mouse.

"Once more unto the breach, dear friends, once more," he murmured as he squeezed through the craggy crevice into the space beyond.

Inside, he found a cavern that went as high as the mountain and as far as he could see. On the floor were wooden cases filled with gold bars. There were clefts in the mountain side where glowing spots blinked on and off all around him like fireflies. He could hear the rushing water outside that threatened to drown out a quiet chattering of click-click-click. Pinkerton held his lamplight up to inspect the glowing glyphs that were carved into the walls. The trolls had clawed beautiful gilded scrolling through the rock and filled it with a mosaic of gold and some sort of fluorescent moss. In four separate places, packed into the stone with such force as to make a small shelf, were four figurines. Pinkerton plucked one out with his Bowie knife. The idol was a strange caricature of a troll with flowing hair and long, drooping breasts. The face was strangely serene.

He looked down at the small goddess in his hand. Pinkerton took a step back to see the whole canvas. It was then he could see all the details in the mosaic. Bit of tin. Silver spoons, forks. Leg and arm bones. Rib cages. Handfuls of teeth. Tufts of scalps with hair.

This is a temple. But to what?

His thought was interrupted as a sharp talon grabbed Pinkerton by the shoulder and slammed him to the ground. The golden goddess fell out of his hand, rolled and smashed into the wall. The creature screeched at the blasphemy, jumped on his back and began clawing viciously at Pinkerton, tearing at his back and head.

Pinkerton crawled away and flipped onto his back. The troll that came at him was female, like the small fetishes, with swaying, bulbous breasts tattooed with gold. On its head, it wore a crown of curly red hair braided with gold and the strange glowing moss. Pinkerton's heart skipped a beat when he realized the wig was made from a blood clotted leathery scalp glued down with mud and fungus. The troll advanced, screaming a spine curdling shriek and pinned Pinkerton down.

Chapter Nineteen

"What's with those tin stars, boys?" asked the Sheriff.

"We've been deputized," said Larry.

"Yeah, we're bonafied!" said Enoch.

"Pinkertons can go to hell." Mooneyham grimaced as he readjusted himself in the saddle. "Where are Garrett and Juan?"

"What's left of them is just over there," said Larry.

"I told you! I told you!" Mayor Brown's voice raised an octave. "Your hubris will take us all down, Mooneyham!"

"Shut up, fool!" Talley hissed.

"Where is Pinkerton?" asked Mooneyham.

"Inside the mountain," said Enoch. "Getting the gold. After that, he's going to blow the whole thing up."

"Son of a bitch!" exclaimed Talley. "Son of a bitch! We're ruined!"

"And because of that, more blood will need to be spilled," Mooneyham shook his head.

The sheriff dropped his horse's rein and stepped forward.

"It's a damn shame you chose the wrong side, boys." Sherriff Mulligan pulled back the hammer on his pistol.

"Whoa! Whoa!" Enoch held his hands up and took a step back. "I won't say nothing. I didn't hear anything!"

"Sorry, boys." Mulligan took aim. "It's hard to find good help these days."

"To hell with that! I quit!" There was the sound of a match flaring to life and then the crackle of a sparkler igniting. The smell of sulfur filled the air as Larry threw a handful of lit sparklers towards the former boss.

"What the hell is that?" said the Sheriff.

"Come on!" Larry grabbed Enoch's arm and fled away from the snapping sparklers and the shadows that were flooding from the rocks.

The sounds of snippy clicker clacks like cicadas, low at first but growing louder very, very quickly enveloped the men.

"Holy hell! *Run!!*" screamed the Sheriff. He grappled with his saddle's pommel as he tried to mount the poor creature. The horse bucked, knocking the Sheriff to the ground, kicking him in the gut as it ran away.

The other horses, taking its cue also reared and tossed off the Mayor and Mooneyham, leaving them to their fates.

The banker, Talley, unfortunately caught his foot in the stirrup and was dragged away by the terrified horse. His screams added fire to the horse's panic and made it run even faster. His body slapped the ground like a rag doll, his limbs flapping like an injured bird until he screamed no more.

The three men, now horseless, were left to stand their ground.

"Gentlemen, I want to take this moment to say that it's been an honor to serve as your Mayor," said Darryl "Toad" Brown.

"Oh, shut up, you stupid sack of pansy shit!" shouted the Sheriff.

"Do as you all will but I'll be damned if I die this way," said Mooneyham. "I will be the architect of my demise." He put the barrel of his gun into his mouth and blasted a bullet into his brain.

After his body fell to the ground, the cacophony of chittering swelled and overwhelmed the screams and bullets of the men left behind.

Chapter Twenty

The troll reared back, showing rows and rows of jagged fangs. As it prepared for the death strike, Pinkerton slashed out with his Bowie knife, slicing through the thing's neck.

Cold, gray, brackish water gushed out of the wound, drenching Pinkerton. The troll rolled off him, gagging and slashing its long talons into the stone. Its death cries alerted others and they crawled out of the crevices and cracks. Dozens of her followers rushed out from the craggy holes to her aid. Males screeched and bared their rows of fangs, beating their chests as they advanced toward their enemy. Females squatted and swayed, wailing a death song as they circled around their priestess and cried out to their gods as her life slowly seeped away. Small faces of children peeked out in wonder at the drama happening below.

Pinkerton crawled on his knees and vomited up the troll blood. Upon hearing this, the creatures screeched and howled at the sacrilege. He looked at the congregation as they slowly creeped towards him and then over at the wooden cases and the gold bars.

"To hell with it. Let the bastards have it." He got to his feet and ran. The trolls started after him like hounds on a fox.

He squeezed through the crevice as wet, fungus laden claws snatched at his legs, hooking through his pants as they tried to pull him back like a fish on a line. He kicked and screamed at the gray, pug-nosed faces but his foot melted into the squishy flesh. "Let go, you ugly bastards!" He reached around and slashed with his Bowie knife until it relinquished his leg.

He fell on his ass and as he pulled free. The trolls spilled out of the wall like roaches in a dirty kitchen. He scrambled back to his feet and didn't stop to look back. The bridge creaked and the rotten wood beneath his feet snapped and broke beneath his weight. He kept running, barely staying one slat ahead as the bridge fell to decay.

Chapter Twenty One

Sigerson stood by the plunger, tapping his foot. His attention wavered between his pocket watch and the tunnel. Fifteen minutes had passed since he lost sight of Pinkerton going into the darkness.

His heartbeat quickening as the minutes counted down.

Fourteen.

The sounds of boots frantically slapping the hard ground to his left caught his attention. It was Larry and Enoch and they were running towards him as if the devil was closing in on them.

"They're coming!" The young men shouted. "They are coming! Blow it up! Blow it up now!"

Sigerson checked the time. *Ten minutes...no, nine.*

"What the hell are you waiting for?" said Enoch.

Larry stopped and leaned over, his hands on his knobby knees, as he struggled to catch his breath in the dusty air. "Did you hear us? Those sons of bitches are coming this way! Blow it up!"

"Not yet," replied Sigerson.

"Look, the old guy is dead," argued Enoch. "And we're going to be soon if don't push that plunger!"

Enoch reached for the device but Sigerson, who towered over him, stared the man down.

"He has three," he said, checking his timepiece. "Two minutes left."

"But do we?!?!?"

Just then, a drenched, bloody figure came running out from the tunnel.

"BLOW IT UP!" shouted Pinkerton. "SIGERSON, BLOW IT UP NOW!"

Sigerson wanted to wait a few seconds longer to guarantee his boss' safety but as soon as the first gray, pug nosed face breached from the mouth of the tunnel, he slammed the plunger down.

Nothing happened.

Sigerson looked to Larry and Enoch for answers.

"Don't look at us!"

"One of those sons of bitches must've knocked loose a wire!"

"Dammit! Hand me your Winchester."

Enoch handed over his gun and Sigerson took careful aim at a stick of dynamite jutting from the lip of the tunnel. He took a deep breath, exhaled and pulled the trigger.

There was a brief, torturous second before the bullet reacted with the unstable, sweating dynamite and then a very loud explosion as every stick went off in a chain reaction.

The rolling shock waves sent the running Pinkerton flying through the air. He came down to the earth and rolled a half a dozen turns, landing, bruised and dazed, near Sigerson. The horses faired only slightly better as the blast frightened them into a frenzied stampede away from the dust and chaos. The trolls' chitter chattering screams reached a crescendo as the tunnel fell in on itself and sealed it off forever.

"Boss!" Sigerson dropped Thor and ran to Pinkerton. Larry and Enoch followed close behind.

"I'm fine!" The older man shooed them away. "Is it done? Are they still following me?"

"No, the coast is clear," he said, helping Pinkerton to his feet. "Looks like we closed it off. I don't think the Elixir Spa is going to be pleased."

"Damn the spa and all those snake oil bastards," said Pinkerton. "Where are the horses?"

"They ran off. I doubt they went too far."

"Wait! It looks like the horses are coming back!" said Enoch.

"Well, that's a spot of good luck for us, I'd say!" said Sigerson.

Pinkerton squinted at the rushing thundering dust cloud coming towards them. "Unless you ask the question: Why?"

Chapter Twenty-Two

The screaming troll faces in the rolling dust storm kicked up by the three terrified horses revealed the answer to Pinkerton's question.

"What the hell is that?" said Sigerson.

"What we were telling you about!" said Larry.

"The ones from the ridge!" Enoch ran his hands through his dusty hair. "Oh, hell! What do we do now?"

"Men, prepare yourselves!" Pinkerton shouted as he reached for his Bowie knife. "Sigerson, hand me my pistol. How soon can you get Thor ready for another volley?"

"No can do, sir. The rest of my ammunition just ran past us on my horse."

"What?" said Enoch. "Are you saying all we have is our pistols and our knives? We are screwed!"

"We still have breath, we can still fight. Sigerson, take Larry and catch that horse," said Pinkerton. "Enoch, come with me."

"Where to?"

"Into battle." He slapped the young man on the shoulder. "Time to earn that badge."

"Is it too late to give it back?"

****

Sigerson stopped and looked back at Pinkerton. He stood as solid as a wall that would not be moved. He couldn't shake the feeling the trumpets were readying to shake down Jericho.

Larry grabbed his arm. "Come on, that horse isn't getting any slower."

"Godspeed, boss," he muttered and ran with Larry after the speeding horse.

****

There were six trolls in the first wave. They were small, weak and fell easily under Pinkerton's blade. Enoch preferred a more long-distance method of execution and wasted four bullets on two of the creatures.

As the dust settled, the second legion of a two dozen trolls could be seen standing in a line. Their heads were lowered so their eyes took on the look of a hooded snake. Their chests heaved with anger and blood lust. Half of them held long staves with sharpened rocks on their tips, the rest clenched and unclenched their claws, their long talons clicking in frustration.

"Save those bullets, kid," said Pinkerton. "That first batch was fodder to make us waste our ammunition."

"Are you saying these things can think?"

"I saw a temple inside that tunnel. There was an altar made of bone, hair and gold."

"That's crazy! What the hell do they pray to?"

A long wail broke out, coming as if from the heavens and drew the men's eyes skyward. Standing on a wayward boulder, stood a troll. She was naked, as they all were, her breasts swollen and swaying, between them embedded in her sternum was a golden amulet. Her skin was tattooed even more elaborately than the one Pinkerton had killed in the tunnel. Golden swirls carved through her gray, soft, fungoid skin and sparkled in the dying sunlight. The long blonde scalped tresses she wore as a tiara exploded against the pink and purple tinged sunset.

She lifted a staff that dangled human leg bones like a macabre wind chime and threw back her bulbous head to scream. She opened her mouth so wide it seemed her jaws would unhinge and shrieked out an unintelligible war cry. Her tongue jutted out, spiking the air as horrible, guttural burps and growls vomited out what passed for a language. The sound echoed and chilled the blood of the men below. Deep inside, somewhere where the first fears of our ancestors still dwell, an alarm sounded. The hairs on the back of their necks bristled and they all had to resist the urge to turn away and just run.

"Wh-what is hell is that?" Enoch sputtered.

"I think we just met their god," said
Pinkerton. "And she's the vengeful sort."

Chapter Twenty-Three

Sigerson and Larry caught a break as the horses were stopped by two unstoppable forces: a mountain ridge and the temptation of a cold drink from the man-made lake of the Elixir Spa spring water.

The horses lifted their heads as the two men approached.

"Be still. We don't want to set them off." Sigerson grabbed Larry's shoulder. "That white mare. See her? She has my haversack."

The two men took a step forward and the horses reared and snorted in alarm. They all stamped on the ground, nervous and ready to bolt.

"Do you have any food?" asked Sigerson.

"Do I look like someone who carries horse treats in my pocket?" asked Larry.

"Damn, we need some kind of bait. Wait!" Sigerson remembered the honey slathered biscuit. He pulled the handkerchief with the half-smashed gift from his pocket.

Sigerson gave Thor to Larry as he slowly approached the anxious beast, muttering soft assurances.

"Here you go, girl. It's okay. Shhh, shhhh. It's okay."

He reached her, put the sweet treat to her muzzle and while she chewed, he quickly retrieved his haversack from the pommel, and grabbed the remaining fourteen cartridges. Sigerson held them up in triumph.

"Yes!" Larry let out a breath of relief.

Just then an inhuman scream reverberated through the air, bouncing off the rocks as if threatening to bring down the entire mountain. Sigerson gripped his horse's bridle and pulled her to himself as the other horses bolted away.

"Oh, no, my friend. It's time to earn that biscuit." He hoisted himself onto the saddle, gripped her sides with his muscular thighs and guided her towards Larry.

"Give me Thor," he said.

Larry held the gun up to Sigerson who sheathed it in a specially built holster. He held his hand out, "Come on up! We need to ride!"

Chapter Twenty-Four

"Holy Christ, holy Christ, holy Christ!" Enoch stammered.

"Steady yourself, son. Keep at my back. We'll fight as one."

"What the hell is that? *What the hell is that?*"

"Stick behind me like glue, boy, back to back." Pinkerton reached back and grabbed the terrified man's arm. "That way none of them can get behind either of us. Understand me?"
Enoch garbled something.

"I didn't hear you. *Do you understand me?*"

"I do! I do!"

The Troll Queen screamed her war cry again and the warriors approached slowly, menacingly. As if they wanted the terror in their prey to season the meat for the feast.

"Get ready for the fight of your life."

Pinkerton checked that there were six bullets in the chambers, holstered it, gripped his Bowie knife, and bared his teeth in a fierce smile.

One troll, wearing a gold circlet around his thick neck, peeled off from the pack, returned the grimace and rushed at him with his stone tipped spear. Pinkerton parried the stick with the Bowie, grabbed it and pulled the brute in close enough to stab it through the neck. Fetid water rushed out and the creature fell over, gagging.

Pinkerton snapped the spear over his knee and growled in glee.

"Boss, what the hell are you doing?" muttered Enoch.

"Taking control of the situation," he replied. He beat his chest and roared, "Come at me, you ugly sons of bitches! What are you waiting for? Come at me!"

The troll queen standing on the rock top, shook her staff, made a shrill, whirling whistle sound and shrieked out a command.

The rest of the troop picked up her war cry and descended like banshees.

Pinkerton aimed and took down two with his pistol. The noise startled two others who retreated but quickly return to the melee.

Enoch shot wildly into the crowd, tagging one in the shoulder and catching another one right between the eyes.

"Save your bullets, you damn fool!" shouted Pinkerton.

"I'm more worried about saving my damn skin!" Enoch popped off three more bullets, knee capping one, winging another and the last bullet slamming into the rocks beyond.

"Shit! I'm out!" A troll lunged at Enoch and he pistol whipped the pug-nosed abomination in the face. He pulled out his Arkansas Toothpick and jabbed at the injured troll, stabbing it in the eye. It screamed and fell, writhing on the ground.

Pinkerton slashed out with his Bowie knife to give him room to aim his pistol. Two more bullets left their chambers and entered the craniums of his targets. He turned to face two more trolls, waving his Bowie knife and they retreated, screeching loudly in fear.

"Show off," said Enoch.

A troll with only one arm slid up in all the confusion and stabbed Enoch in the thigh with his spear.

"Goddammit!" Enoch yelled out. "Son of a bitch snuck up on me!"

The beast made a shrill cry of victory and leaned in, thrusting the spear deeper into the muscle and twisted the shaft. Enoch to dropped to the ground in agony.

"Enoch!" Pinkerton turned to see the young man fall and three wounded trolls descend on him.

"Sons of bitches!" he yelled and took aim at the feasting fiends.

Two trolls took advantage and jumped on Pinkerton's back. The sudden jolt ruined his aim causing him to fire into the chaos hitting one troll in the back and the other bullet finding a home in Enoch's chest.

Anger flared inside Pinkerton as he saw the young man go limp and the fiends begin to messily feast on his body. Another troll joined in and the weight of all three brought him to the ground causing him to drop his pistol. He held onto his Bowie knife and attempted to wriggle out of the dogpile but the largest of the brutes pinned him down with a sharp talon through his shoulder. The hilt of the knife cut into Pinkerton. He grimaced, biting back the agony as the troll slowly turned the claw inside the wound.

The troll queen descended from her high ground. As she walked towards the downed prisoner, the remaining trolls, living or injured, prostrated themselves before her. She kicked aside one or two of the more injured warriors, displeased by their performance and made a *chikchikchik* sound. They cowered ever more and pulled themselves off the field of battle.

The troll that stood over the prisoner lowered his head and the troll queen purred as she laid her hand on its gray dome and carved out a sigil in the puffy skin. Pinkerton felt the hot water splash onto his back as it poured from the wound.

She made a clicking noise with her tongue and the honoured warrior pulled his talon from the prisoner. Pinkerton did his best to stifle a scream as the jagged nail ripped out of his back.

The troll queen loomed over him. The leg bones rattled as she balanced her grotesque girth with the staff. The smell of brine and rotting flesh from the tiara descended like a heavy, nauseating miasma. She reached down, grabbed him by the hair and pulled him up to his knees. Pinkerton did not resist. He held the knife against his forearm, praying that she did not notice the glint of the blade. She squatted, and her bulbous tattooed breasts swayed and covered her exposed womanhood. She stared in curiosity at his thick salt and pepper beard and pricked at it with her talon. She then traced her own face, measuring her flabby chin for a fit. A smile slid across her face. Yes, this new piece would indeed be a good fit for a queen.

She placed her claw on his cheek near his ear and began to carve off her prize.

This time, Pinkerton didn't hold back the scream.

It was soon drowned out by a sudden roar of thunder and the splash of brains as the honoured warrior's head exploded.

"I am Agent Lothar Sigerson of the Pinkerton Agency," Sigerson said, balancing Thor on his shoulder. Larry took aim with his Winchester at the troll queen's head. "And I ask you, politely, to take your hands off my boss."

Chapter Twenty-Five

The troll queen tore her claw from the prisoner's face and tossed him aside. She held her staff aloft and pointed her gnarled talon towards Sigerson and screeched out a command to attack.

The troll troops rushed out even though her cry was cut short as Pinkerton rose up to his knees and thrust his Bowie knife deep inside her gut.

She screamed and threw her staff away. Spittle drooled off her fat lips and fell on his face as she swiped at Pinkerton with both claws, raking his face and shoulders. He pushed the knife in further, releasing a torrent of sour salty water. She threw her head back in frustration, howled and then turned her attention to his arms, grabbing them tightly within her talons until blood stained the white shirtsleeves red.

His arms quaked with exhaustion as she used her strength to slowly pull the knife free.

****

A screaming horde of trolls, some wounded and dragging their limbs, others full and hardy, rushed towards Sigerson and Larry.

"Conserve your bullets but focus on the front line," said Sigerson.

Larry took aim. "This is going to be a piece of cake." He pulled the hammer back and prepared to take a shot when he saw something familiar lying in a heap on the ground.

"Enoch?"

Two trolls were fighting over his body, tearing it to shreds. Enoch's head rolled to the side and kept on rolling away as the creatures fought over the shredded remainders.

"What the hell? Enoch!" Larry ran toward his fallen brother, blasting out his arrival.

"Larry, what are you doing….no!" Sigerson ran after him.

Larry's rifle clicked empty. "Get off him you sons of bitches!" he yelled as he pulled out his blade.

The trolls jumped back, out of reach and circled around the grieving young man.

"Jesus, what did they do to you, Enoch?" He fell to his knees beside the body. "What am I going to tell Ma? Christ in heaven, you're all eat up!"

Sigerson swung Thor like a hammer, keeping the circling trolls in his sight and stood over Larry. "Get up. Hear me? Get up! We have to move."

"But, look at him. He's all ate up."

"It's going to be the same for us and I don't fancy that for an ending so get up!"

Just then, a troll with an arm snapped off at the elbow snarled and leapt.

****

Pinkerton took a deep breath, set his jaw firmly and struggled to right himself. He ignored the fiery pain in his arms and shoulders and kept his eyes fixed on the hellish face in front of him.

Stand up, you bastard, STAND UP!

On his feet, he held firm and dragged the knife upwards. *There has to be a heart somewhere!*

She reared back from the pain as Pinkerton sliced until the blade hit something hard and became stuck in between her flailing breasts.

The amulet.

"Shit!"

The troll queen's lips tore back into a toothy grin and she wrapped her talons around his neck.

****

The one-armed troll chittered and screamed as it jumped onto the giant's shoulders

Its left arm ended in a gnarled stump, healed from some long-ago injury, so it held onto its mount with teeth and remaining claws. It chomped down on Sigerson's left ear and stabbed his right shoulder.

"Aaaargh! For the love of GOD! GET IT OFF!" Sigerson dropped his beloved Thor and twirled like a frenzied dervish, frantically grabbing at the biting nuisance. The troll shifted from shoulder to shoulder, keeping just out of reach until his back was slick with blood.

The plight of his new partner broke through Larry's grief and he jumped at the chance for some revenge. He grabbed at the troll and peeled it off Sigerson's back and slammed it to the ground. He unsheathed his Arkansas Toothpick, a slender blade with a rough reputation and stabbed the creature through its shoulder, pinning it to the rough ground, screaming, "Die, die, die! You goddamn son of a bitch! DIE!"

The noise aroused the interest of other trolls and they ran towards the spectacle.

"You bastards! COME AND GET IT!" he pulled his knife out of the troll who scurried away as soon as it was free. Larry kicked dirt after the retreating foe. "That's right! Run, you little shit!"

"They are everywhere!" yelled Sigerson, joining the fight.

"Good! Makes it easier to kill them!"

Larry yelled and ran into the coming horde. He was a frenzied whirlwind, kicking one like a wild bronco and slashing at another, but it was all for nothing. The monsters would rebound just as fast as they went down.

Soon, they were both overwhelmed as the gray, pig-faced horde dragged them down under a pile.

****

She made a wet purring sound and pressed her face towards his as her claws tightened around Pinkerton's throat.

He sneered and smashed his forehead into what would be a nose on a normal woman. The force drove her backwards and Pinkerton fell with her, landed unceremoniously on top. It felt as if she were a squishy block of moldy cheese. The amulet stayed in place, keeping the blade from moving. He groaned in disgust but kept death grip on the hilt of the Bowie knife. He struggled but even from this angle, the blade wasn't going to cut through the metal amulet lodged in flesh and bone.

So be it.

If you can't go up…

Go under.

Pinkerton sat up, pulled his Bowie knife out and plunged his fist into the slit and reached upwards. The troll queen arced her back and bucked feebly as his hand found her heart, clutched onto the meaty organ, twisting it and squeezing it until it popped like an over ripe tomato in his fist.

The troll queen shuddered once more and then flattened beneath Pinkerton. He jumped up and removed his arm from her chest, grimacing to hold back the bile that was rising in his throat. His entire arm was covered in a yellow black goop that dripped off in thick, buttery glops. He stepped shakily away from the corpse. Nausea, exhaustion and the total insanity of the last hour came crashing down on him.

Over his shoulder, he heard Larry yell, "You bastards! COME AND GET IT!"

He turned in time to see Sigerson joining the melee, only to fall and be overwhelmed.

"Shit!" he grunted and looked around for a weapon. The hilt of his Bowie jutted from the troll queen's chest. He grabbed it with both hands and yanked as if it were Excalibur in the stone.

He started towards the fight but was arrested by thought: What good is one blunted knife against a bloodthirsty throng of cannibals?

He didn't need a pencil to figure out those odds.

"Damn!" He scanned the ground for the hope of a dropped gun or rifle. All around were bodies of trolls and their queen but not one gun to be seen.

He had nothing he could use to fight them! There was nothing but his knife and–

And then a grisly idea popped into his head.

****

The trolls ripped and tore at him as they piled on, but he had stopped feeling pain. As the weight of the pack crushed every bit of air from his lungs, Sigerson focused everything he had left on breathing. Over the troll's squelching cries, he could still hear Larry blasting out curses on God and everything holy. Strangely, the blasphemy comforted him as cool blackness tinged the corners of his consciousness. *Perhaps Larry will get out of this alive…*

A high pitched shrill whistle drilled into his eardrum and brought Sigerson back from the brink. "Lookey, lookey what I have here," Pinkerton yelled. "Take a good look, you godforsaken, hellish troglodytes!"

Precious oxygen flooded back into his lungs and the trolls jumped off Sigerson's back. He struggled up to his hands and knees, coughing on the dirt that clogged his nose and throat, and heard Larry sputter, "What…the…holy…*hell*?!"

Sigerson lifted his head and saw Pinkerton, a broad, tooth smile on his face, his arms streaked in black yellow bile and holding aloft, spiked on the troll queen's staff, the aforementioned royal's head. The trolls gathered around Pinkerton in a half moon crescent formation. None of them approached any closer, all of them keeping a respectful three-foot radius as they wailed, ripped their claws at their breasts and mourned for their dead queen.

"You want it?" asked Pinkerton. "Is that what you want?"

The trolls' wails increased as they implored for the remains.

"All right then." Pinkerton pulled the staff from the ground and tossed it like a macabre javelin. The trolls all chased after the relic, squabbling and pulling at each other, as they raced to be the first to capture it.

"Are you going to let those bastards live?" said Larry. "After what they did?"

Pinkerton shrugged. "What we came for is lost in that mountain. If you want to carry on, that is up to you, Deputy, but first, I'll need you to hand over that badge. You do that on your own time."

Larry unpinned the badge and threw it on the ground. "They killed my brother. I'm going to go give him a Christian burial and then I'm going to kill every last one of them!" The young man found his rifle among the carnage and ran off after the retreating trolls.

Sigerson picked up the badge and slipped into his pocket. "You all right, boss?"

"I'm fine, Agent. See if you can round up the horses. I want to get the hell out of here."

"Will do."

Pinkerton sat down on a rock to catch his breath. What he had thought was a simple highwayman situation had twisted and turned into something he had never, ever imagined. He was a man who saw the world in black and white. Crime and punishment. Where was the justice in this? A chittering sound to his left alerted him and he moved quickly to the right. A dying troll swiped out at Pinkerton. The gnarled scarred stump of his left arm hung at its side, useless.

"Still got a fight in you, is that right?"

The troll growled in exhausted defiance and spit black blood at Pinkerton's feet.

Remembering the old drunk's story, Pinkerton unsheathed his Bowie knife, ended the creature's misery and cut off its head as a souvenir.

It wasn't gold but, for Gibson, it would be enough.

THE END

ABOUT THE AUTHOR

Nikki Nelson-Hicks has always been more of a
Black Hat gal.

www.ingramcontent.com/pod-product-compliance
Lightning Source LLC
Chambersburg PA
CBHW050743230626
47052CB00004BA/1108